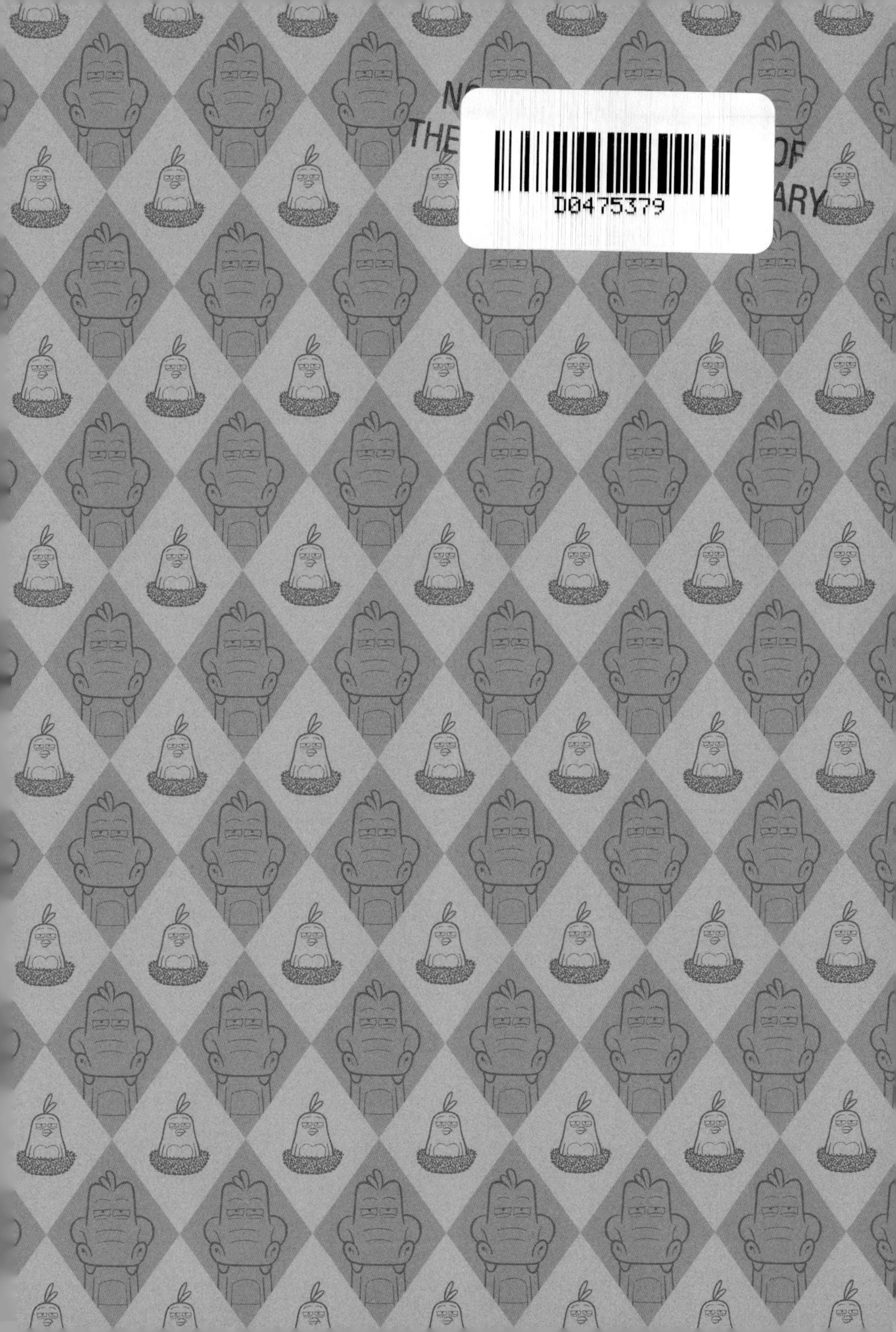
D0475379

Norm Feuti

An Imprint of HarperCollinsPublishers

For Charlotte and Ben

HarperAlley is an imprint of HarperCollins Publishers.

Beak & Ally #2: Bedtime Jitters

For information address HarperCollins Children's Books, a division of HarperCollins Publishers, 195 Broadway, New York, NY 10007.
www.harperalley.com

Library of Congress Control Number: 2021931869
ISBN 978-0-06-302160-0

Typography by Norm Feuti
21 22 23 24 25 GPS 10 9 8 7 6 5 4 3 2 1

First Edition

One
Ally

Ahh! There's nothing like being alone with a good book on a quiet day.

Hi, Ally!

Hello, Beak.

What are you reading?

It's called *Inspiring Alligators through History.*

Ooooooh! Sounds interesting.

Are there any stories about inspiring **birds** in there?
I doubt it.
You never know. Birds have done **a lot** of inspiring things.

Like Alexander Birdington, the first Secretary of the Worm Treasury.

Or Wilbur and Orville Swallow, the first birds to carry a coconut across the Atlantic.

Or Feathers "Red Bottom" McGee, the original badminton birdie.

Or Neil Wingstrong, the first bird to go to the moon!

3...2...1...

Although that was more of an accident.
Beak...
Do you need something? Because I'd **really** like to get back to my book. 
Oh, right...

I forgot. You like your alone time.
That's right.

Sorry.
It's okay.

I **have** to remind myself: Ally likes her alone time.

Yes. Yes, she does.

Soooo?
What?

Do you **need** something?!
Oh, right! I almost forgot why I came here.

There's some by that tree over there. Help yourself.

I see it. Thanks, Ally!

Oh, yes. This is very nice.

Hrrrngh!

Hrrrrngh!

Hrrrnngh!

Hrrrnngh!

Hrrrnngh!

Hrrrrrrrnnnnnngh!

Huff
Huff
I think it's stuck.
Here, let me do it.

I insist.

Oh, you don't have to--

Thanks, Ally. You're a good friend.

Yes, well, let's just finish up with the moss.

I'm desperate for a good night's sleep. I've been hearing strange noises at night.

Weird noises.

Yes, the swamp is like that.

Scary noises.

Well, I'm sure the moss will do the trick. I'm going back to my book.

Two

This moss **is** nice and comfy.

Maybe it will be all I need to...

Yawn

...get a good night's...

... sleep.

Snore

ZZZUMP

Oh my!
What was
that?!

ZZUMP
There
it is
again!

ZZUMP
ZZUMP
What
is
that?!

What if it's a hideous monster?!

A hideous **robot** monster...

... that **flies** and breathes **fire** ...

... and eats **birds** in a **single bite**?!

And n-now it s-sounds like it's r-right under my t-t-t-tree!

ZZZUMP
ZZZUMP

Splash

Eeeeep!

It's after me!
FLAP FLAP
FLAP
FLAP FLAP

ZZZZZ
Ally

Save me, Ally!
WHOMP!

What the ... Who?! What's going on?!
It's after me!

Ally

The swamp is full of monsters, Ally! And each one has its own terrifying call!

There's the horrible Grunty Beast!
GUURNT GUURNT!
And the chilling Chatter Ghosts!
CHH CHH CHH CHH!
And now the mechanical Zump Monster!
ZZUMP ZZUMP!

There are no such things as monsters, Beak.
Ally
I hear them every night!

The swamp is filled with strange noises. You get used to it.

Monsters aren't something I can get **used** to!

Ally

There **are** no monsters.

That's just what the monsters **want** you to think!

Ally

Beak, it's very late. Why don't I walk you back to your nest?

No! I can't go back there!

You really don't.
Let me grab some more of that moss to sleep on.

PLOP

Yawn! I'm exhausted.

Snoooork!

Fee Boo
Boo Boo
Boo Boo

Snooork!
♪ Fee Boo ♪
♪ Boo Boo
♪ Boo Boo ♪
Ally

Ally

Finally, a good night's sleep.
That makes one of us.
Thank you for letting me stay here, Ally. 
Mm-hmm.

But don't worry. I won't need to sleep on top of your head tonight.
Good.

If I start building a new nest now, I should have it finished by nighttime.

New nest?! Where?!
In your tree, of course.

No, no, no. Absolutely not.
But I **need** to stay here until the monsters move away!

There are no monsters, Beak. And I'm going to prove it to you.

Tonight, I'll show you what all the swamp noises are. Then you'll **know** there are no monsters.
You'd do that for **me**?

Fee Boo
Fee Boo
Fee Boo
Fee Boo
For you? Sure.
You're such a good friend, Ally.
Ally

Three

What if there are no noises in the swamp tonight?

Why wouldn't there be?

The monsters might be scared off because you're here.

There are no monsters, Beak.

The **Zump Monster**! Can't you hear it?!

ZZUMP ZZUMP ZZUMP

All I can hear is a bullfrog.

Bullfrog?
That's what that noise is.

Are you sure?
Come with me. I'll show you.

What if you're wrong?
Trust me. You'll be fine.

ZZUMP
ZZUMP
ZZUMP

See?
ZZUMP
ZZUMP

It **is** just a frog!
I told you there was no Zump Monster.
Splash

I'm so relieved!
Great! Problem solved! I'll drop you off at your nest and we can both get some sleep.

But wait! What about the Chatter Ghosts and the Grunty Beast?
Oh, brother.

CHH CHH CHH CHH CHH CHH
Gasp! There they are right now! The Chatter Ghosts!
Those are cicadas.

CHH CHH CHH CHH CHH CH

Whatever they're called, they're **everywhere**!

Of course they are. The swamp is **filled** with bugs.

CHH CHH CHH CHH CHH CH

Cicadas are **bugs**?

Come. I'll show you.

Well, that's ridiculous. No self-respecting bird is afraid of a **bug**.

I agree. It **is** ridiculous. Can we go home now?

You still haven't explained the Grunty Beast. That's the most horrible-sounding creature of all.
Fine. Let's listen.

GUUURNT GURNT
GURNT GUUUURNT

There it is!

GUUURNT
GURNT GURNT
That's a heron. They make some strange noises.
I was scared of a fellow **bird**?!

RRRRRRRRRRRRRRRRRRR

I got all worked up over nothing.

RRRRRRRRRRRRRRRRR

I suppose that noise is something harmless too.

Um.

RRRRRRRRRRRRRRRRR

It's probably just a swamp mushroom or something, right?

Mushrooms don't make noise.

RRRRRRRRRRRRRRRRRRRRR
Then what is it?
Actually, I don't know **what** that noise is.
RRRRRRRRRRRRRRRRRRRRR
But maybe we should find out.
Wait, what?

RRRRRRRRRRRRRRRRRRRRR

You sure about this?
Yeah.
I hope we don't run into any rangers. 
Quit worrying and help me with the tailgate.

The quicker we dump this garbage, the sooner we can get out of here.

Gasp! Those humans are going to dump **trash** in our swamp!

Whisper
Whisper
Whisper

Let's dump this first. Help me lift it.

Fee Boo Fee Boo Fee Boo

Do you hear that?

Fee Boo Fee Boo Fee Boo Fee Boo

I think it's a siren.

Maybe it's just an ambulance.

Fee Boo Fee Boo Fee Boo

It sounds like it's getting closer!

Fee Boo Fee Boo Fee Boo

Splash Splash Splash

Fee Boo Fee Boo Fee Boo

Splash Splash Splash Splash

Someone's coming!

It's the **rangers**! Somebody must have told on us! Let's get out of here!

RRRRRRRRRRRRR
It worked!

Scary noises for the win!
Well done, Beak! You saved the swamp!

And I guess we have your **bedtime jitters** to thank for it. We wouldn't have been out here otherwise.

We make a good team.
I suppose we do.

Come on. Let's head home.

Should we have another sleepover, just for fun?
I think I've had enough fun for one night.

Want more Beak & Ally? Check out...